Hands as Warm as Toast

by Lisa Himle
illustrations by Bruce Langton

mitten press

All inquiries should be addressed to:

Mitten Press

An imprint of Ann Arbor Media Group LLC

2500 S. State Street

Ann Arbor, MI 48104

Printed and bound in China.

10   9   8   7   6   5   4   3   2   1

Library of Congress Cataloging Data on File.

ISBN-13: 978-1-58726-298-2

ISBN-10: 1-58726-298-3

Book and jacket design by Somberg Design

www.sombergdesign.com

"Momma, I don't want to start kindergarten today," whimpered Libby.

"Why not?" Mother asked.

"I don't know... My backpack is ready to go, but I'm not. My hands are wet and sticky and my throat feels like there's toast stuck in it!"

"Sweetheart, you're just a little nervous." Mother lifted Libby's chin and looked into her wet eyes. "Listen to me. You are smart and kind. You'll do great in kindergarten!"

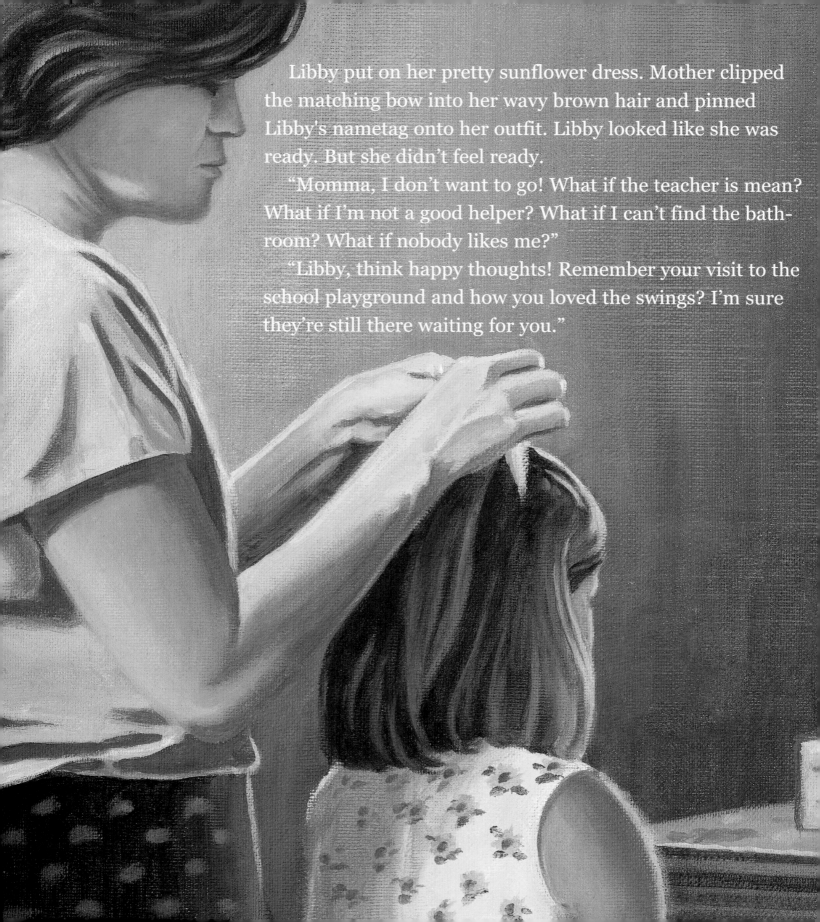

Libby put on her pretty sunflower dress. Mother clipped the matching bow into her wavy brown hair and pinned Libby's nametag onto her outfit. Libby looked like she was ready. But she didn't feel ready.

"Momma, I don't want to go! What if the teacher is mean? What if I'm not a good helper? What if I can't find the bathroom? What if nobody likes me?"

"Libby, think happy thoughts! Remember your visit to the school playground and how you loved the swings? I'm sure they're still there waiting for you."

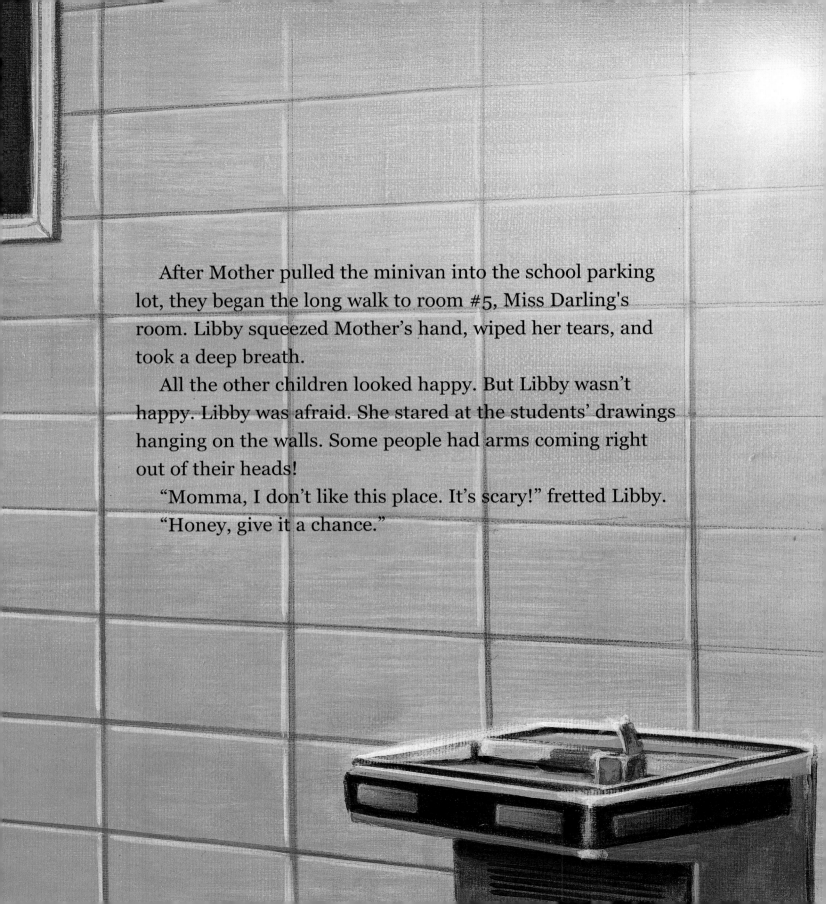

After Mother pulled the minivan into the school parking lot, they began the long walk to room #5, Miss Darling's room. Libby squeezed Mother's hand, wiped her tears, and took a deep breath.

All the other children looked happy. But Libby wasn't happy. Libby was afraid. She stared at the students' drawings hanging on the walls. Some people had arms coming right out of their heads!

"Momma, I don't like this place. It's scary!" fretted Libby.

"Honey, give it a chance."

When they reached room #5, Libby froze. She hid behind her mother's skirt and slowly peeked into the room. She saw some children playing with blocks on the carpet. A few others were snickering and poking the hamster in its cage. "They aren't being very nice," Libby thought to herself.

"Momma, let's go! I've seen kindergarten and I don't like it!"

Just when Libby decided to make a dash for the van, Miss Darling peered around Libby's mother and smiled. Libby looked up at her tall teacher. She wore brown speckled glasses and a pretty flowered skirt. Her blue eyes sparkled when she noticed Libby's nametag.

"Welcome Libby! I've been waiting for you! I have a special job just for you. I was hoping you could warm up my cold hands."

Libby slowly held out her hand.

"Why Libby, your hands are as warm as toast!"said Miss Darling.

A small smile crept across Libby's face.

Mother kissed Libby and waved good-bye. "I'll pick you up by the flagpole. Remember...you have an important job today!"

"Bye, Momma," Libby whispered.

Mother left the room, but after a moment she returned for one last peek. Through the door window, she watched Miss Darling show Libby around the room. Mother took a deep breath, wiped her eyes, and slowly walked away.

Libby held Miss Darling's hand as she showed her the book corner and introduced her to Lauren and Jennifer playing in the kitchen. The girls invited Libby to play with them, but Libby shook her head. She wanted to stay with her teacher. After all, she had a job to do.

It wasn't until recess that Libby was ready to let go. That's when she remembered the swings.

"Are your hands warm enough now?" Libby asked.

"Yes Libby, thanks for keeping my hands so warm today. You're like a little toaster!"

Before she knew it, the bell rang and Libby's first day of kindergarten was over. Mother stood patiently waiting by the flagpole with all the other "pick-up" parents. Libby couldn't run to her fast enough.

"Momma! Miss Darling let me hold her cold hands today. She said my hands were as warm as toast!"

"What a great helper you are! Miss Darling is so lucky that you're in her class," Mother said.

The next day, Miss Darling greeted Libby, "I'm glad you're here! My hands are still cold. Would you like to warm them?"

Every day Libby held on tightly to Miss Darling's hands, but just before recess, she'd ask, "Are your hands warm enough now?"

Miss Darling would always reply, "Yes, thank you, Libby. Your hands are as warm as toast!"

As days turned into weeks, Libby noticed that Miss Darling's hands were warming up much quicker than before. Now her hands were all toasty by snack time instead of staying chilly until recess.

As winter approached, Libby had an idea. Miss Darling's birthday was coming and she wanted to buy her a special present. One afternoon, Libby and Mother went shopping. As Libby passed the hats and scarves, she spied the perfect gift. She gave the money to the shop clerk and quickly wrapped the present when she got home.

The next day Libby bolted into room #5 shouting, "Happy Birthday!!"

Miss Darling's eyes widened as she looked at her present. "I bet you wrapped this all by yourself!"

Inside the box, Miss Darling saw a lovely pair of royal blue mittens trimmed with fuzzy white fur.

"These will keep your hands as warm as toast!" announced Libby.

"Thank you, Libby! I'll think of you whenever I wear them," Miss Darling promised.

Spring followed winter. Libby's kindergarten year was nearing the end. By that time, Libby rarely asked Miss Darling if her hands needed warming. Libby knew the mittens were always in the drawer, just in case.

On the last day of school, Miss Darling gathered the children all around her. One by one, she talked about how special each child was. Libby sat patiently waiting for her turn. Finally Miss Darling said, "Libby...you're so smart and such a wonderful helper. Your hands are as warm as toast!"

Libby was so proud. She hugged Miss Darling and squeezed her hands one last time. "I'll miss you, Miss Darling!"

That summer Libby learned how to do the "Hand Jive" and "Cats' Cradle" with her friends. She also thought a lot about becoming a first grader. This year would be different; Libby KNEW she was ready for first grade.

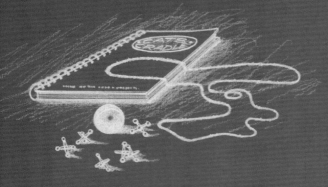

On the first day of school, Libby confi-
dently waved good-bye to Mother in the
school lobby. Libby again noticed the
drawings of people with arms sticking out
of their heads. But this year, she didn't
mind one bit. As she passed the library,
Libby smiled at a teary-eyed girl.

"Hi, I'm Libby. My hands are cold. Would you mind warming them up?"

The kindergartner slowly took Libby's hand.

"Your hands are as warm as toast!" said Libby. The kindergartner smiled.

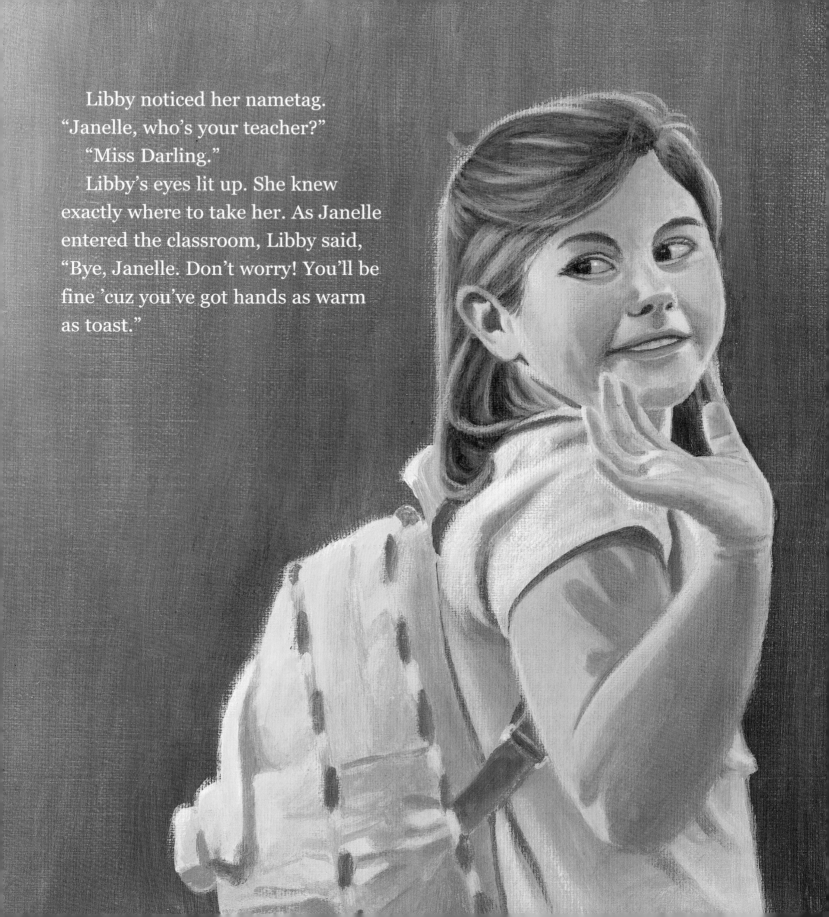

Libby noticed her nametag. "Janelle, who's your teacher?"

"Miss Darling."

Libby's eyes lit up. She knew exactly where to take her. As Janelle entered the classroom, Libby said, "Bye, Janelle. Don't worry! You'll be fine 'cuz you've got hands as warm as toast."

Are **your** hands
as warm as toast?